Disbanding of Disciples

KILLER WORDS PUBLISHING
Cover art by C. L. Conolly

DISBANDING OF DISCIPLES
ISBN - 978-1-963747-00-3

C. L. Conolly
www.clconolly.com
New Ulm, Texas

Printed in the United States of America

10 9 8 7 6 5 4 3 2 1

Disbanding of Disciples

C. L. Conolly

Also written by C. L. Conolly

<u>The Affair Series</u>
Forbidden Affair
Family Affair
Fundamental Affair
Fruitful Affair

<u>Single Titles</u>
Friendly Misfortunes
Killer Suburbia

<u>Cult Series</u>
Disciples Doctrine
City of Disciples
Shunning of Disciples
Mutiny of Disciples
Disbanding of Disciples

The time had come for them to share God's message as taught in the Disciples Doctrine.

One

ive years after his connected partner Omegra's brutal murder, the leader of the disciples was doing everything he could to keep the City of Disciples together. Azril and Omegra's oldest child, Alpha, was in her eighth year and the leader had her assisting with job assignments. She had been assisting the leader since her mother's death. Her father would walk aimlessly through the city without engaging with the disciples.

Since Martin had been assigned as her personal disciple guard, Alpha began leading the worship services by her fifth year. For two years before that Cory, the head disciples guard, was leading the worship services and going over the leadership role with her.

Alpha had been taught how to read a map in order to send out the disciples for recruitment. Even after Azril was able to return to the leader role in the City of Disciples, Cory would still go to Alpha for where he was to take the disciples for recruiting.

Farrah, Martin's connected partner, had been assigned to be Alpha's sister, Juliet's, personal disciples guard. Juliet was six and a half and she was being trained to keep watch over the disciples cultivating the land and taking care of the livestock.

Sara, who had been a part of Omegra's disciples guard, was assigned to Hawk and Sparrow. The twins were days away from their fifth year and Alpha wanted to make sure that her brothers were celebrated as being the masculine heir to the City of Disciples.

Alpha and Juliet had become more confident and looked toward Farrah for a feminine roll model. The girls were in the leader's office preparing to address the disciples after breakfast.

Juliet sat in one of the chairs in front of the desk, across from her sister. "How many disciples are you sending out for recruitment today?"

Alpha sat behind the desk and prepared the job assignments. "Well, I'm having to assign disciples to recruit because Jordan, Vernon, Gerald and Brad have been volunteering to go out every week, but they never bring back any outsiders. They are no longer allowed to leave the city together."

Juliet nodded. "I have seen the four of them skulking around the City of Disciples since Beatrice and Danny had been shunned after the shunning ceremony had been reinstated. When they are together it seems like they are scheming."

Alpha pointed at her sister. "You got that right. I have assigned Tom, Murphy, Warren and David to keep an eye on them. The disciples guard watch the four disciples when they are together, or alone. Although, anytime the disciples guard has been able to get within ear shot of those four disciples when they are congregating together, they stop talking. We haven't been able to gather any information as to what they are planning."

Juliet cocked her head to the side. "But every time they left the city to recruit, they would come

C. L. Conolly

back?"

Alpha nodded. "Yep. Seems fishy, doesn't it?"

Before Juliet could respond, Azril descended the stairs from the leader's living quarters and into the office with Hawk and Sparrow. The boys were pretending to be birds, like their namesakes, and chose to fly around the room, as the leader approached Alpha.

"Sara should be here for the boys soon. I told her that I wanted to spend some time with them this morning." Azril was glad that Hawk and Sparrow had Sara to go to if they needed any kind of motherly figure.

Alpha held her arms out and her brothers 'flew' over to her for a hug. "The boys can hang out for as long as they need to. No rush."

"Well," Azril began. "Cory has been overseeing a project for me and he should be here soon to go over the technical aspects."

Alpha gave her brothers a kiss on their cheeks, then allowed them to 'fly' away. "Are you talking about the recruiting videos online?"

The leader smiled at his oldest daughter. "You are so perceptive. I should have known that you were aware of the new video system."

"Are you putting cameras all over the residential building?" Juliet asked.

"As of right now, they are only in the worship

center in order to livestream the worship services," Azril told his daughter.

"The cameras aren't for surveillance, Juliet," Alpha said, shaking her head.

"Leader, we're ready for you," Cory said as he entered the office.

"I'm on my way. Are all the cameras set up?" Azril asked.

Cory nodded. "Yes sir. Joe and Sean were able to upload the recruiting video and the views have surpassed two hundred thousand."

Azril placed his hand on Alpha's shoulder. "Finish up the job assignments and I'll see you In the worship center." He stepped up to the doors to go out into the worship center and acknowledged his head disciples guard. "How many new disciples have we recruited from the video?"

"At the last count, Sharon informed me that we had received just under three thousand new disciples that had arrived after seeing the video online," Cory told him.

Sara entered the worship center and walked up the aisle toward the leader. "Good morning, Leader."

Azril respectfully lowered his chin and bowed his head to the twins disciples guard. "Good morning, Sara. The boys are in the office with Alpha and Juliet."

Sara bowed her head toward the leader, before heading into the office to get the boys. She made sure to take them out the back entrance in order to not disturb the leader and his disciples guard.

One of the disciples, Skylar, had told Azril how important the internet was to getting attention to the City of Disciples. She had been a disciple for several years and felt as though the recruiting process was slow and daunting. The compensation for recruiting and working within the City of Disciples was more than adequate considering that all of their necessities were taken care of by the leader and all the funds the disciples relinquish to the leader of the disciples as they come to live in the City of Disciples.

The leader agreed and decided that the new recruiting video would be for all outsiders as well as isolated disciples to watch. He wanted to see if the positive message of the Disciples of God was able to be conveyed within the video.

A couple of the isolated disciples had to watch the video three times a day for five days before they were able to be released. Once they were back among the other disciples, they seemed to be completely different. The video worked well enough to turn defectors into loyal disciples.

Since the recruiting video seemed to be working so well, they had begun filming every worship service. If a shunning ceremony was set to commence during the worship service, the video would end with a message to the viewers to join them at the City of Disciples in order to witness the shunning ceremony.

Cory placed his hand on Azril's shoulder. "The cameras are set up in each one of the corners of the worship center in order to get different angles as well as the reactions of the disciples. Our first livestream will be the short morning service before they head out to their job assignments."

The disciples began filing in and Azril headed back into the office to wait for his disciples guard to usher him out. Alpha and Juliet were waiting for him with the job assignments in hand to post for the disciples.

Azril reached out and held hands with his girls. "Martin and Farrah should be in the worship center waiting for the two of you. I appreciate the fact that y'all want to be presented to the disciples with me. Alpha, that is a great leadership quality."

After a few moments, Cory opened the door and the leader emerged out into the worship center with his daughters. The disciples stood and applauded, as he approached the podium. Alpha walked over to the seat where Omegra would sit at the leader's side and joined Martin. Juliet stepped to the other side with Farrah before stepping down off the stage and sitting in the front row. Azril allowed the disciples to cheer for as long as they wanted. Before he started the service, he looked toward Joe and Sean for acknowledgment that the cameras had started and they were live-streaming.

The disciples quieted down and took their seats, just as Joe and Sean pointed at the leader, letting him know they were ready. Azril held his arms out, palms facing the promised land. "Thank you to all loyal disciples, new disciples, followers and outsiders who have joined us here today. God sees you wanting to change your life and your heart. For those of you watching the live video, disciples guard Sean and Joe are ready to answer any of your questions. For those of you here in the City of Disciples, if you have any questions, please use the chain of command, or write your question on the paper provided in the pocket of the pews to place directly into the leader box.

"The reason why I have requested everyone to come in for a mini worship service after breakfast is to inform all the disciples here in the City of Disciples that we are now live-streaming our evening worship services. We have installed speakers in the common area, just outside of the worship center for those of you who would prefer not to be on camera. There are cameras in every corner for every angle.

"I appreciate you joining me this morning. Alpha has your job assignments and once she has them posted, you will be released to go to work. We are disciples of God and we will appease Him in worship."

As the disciples repeated the last line, Alpha walked down the aisle out of the worship center, with Martin close behind her, to mount the job assignments in the residential building.

Two

The only disciples who chose to stay out of the worship center during the evening services was Jordan, Vernon, Gerald and Brad. The four disciples guard that had been assigned to watch them also stayed out in the common area.

The next morning, Tom and Murphy entered the office to report what the disciples had been talking about the night before, as Alpha and Azril were descending the stairs to the office together. The leader's eldest daughter still took each step slowly and carefully, but with less fear each day. Alpha had a fear of the angle of the stairs, being afraid that she would fall down. There were still days when she would ask Azril to carry her down the stairs and he would have her climb on his back.

As she stepped down from the bottom step, Alpha ran over, sat down behind the desk and acknowledged the two disciples guard. "What information do you have for us?"

Tom rubbed the back of his neck and spoke directly to the leader. "Well, last night Jordan seemed to be planning something and we might want to add an extra guard for Alpha."

Azril stepped up behind his daughter and placed his hands on her shoulders. "What do you mean by that? What did he say?"

Murphy took a deep breath. "He basically said that she can't stop them from leaving the City of Disciples to recruit and if they miss another meeting the city could be swarmed."

Alpha looked up at Azril. "Daddy, am I in danger?"

The leader cupped her face in his hands. "No, baby girl. Not only am I here to protect you, but so is Martin and all of the other disciples guard. No one will ever harm you."

"Okay, Daddy." Alpha smiled at Azril, then went to work preparing the job assignments for all of the disciples and followers in the City of Disciples.

Azril ushered Tom and Murphy out to the worship area in order to speak to them privately. "Was there anything else said?"

Tom shook his head. "They noticed that we were listening, so they stopped talking after that. Once the worship service was over, Brad had asked Jordan what they needed to do about Alpha and the job assignments."

Murphy placed his hand on the leader's shoulder. "Jordan told him that he would take care of her. That's why we feel that she may need an extra disciples guard."

Before Azril could respond, Martin entered the worship center and was walking up the aisle toward them. He stopped in front of the leader. "Is everything okay?"

The leader pointed at the door that led into the office. "Get in there and keep an eye on my little girl. Farrah and Sara are upstairs with my other children. I will be sending in another disciples guard to be with you. Alpha is not to be alone for any reason."

Martin just nodded, then rushed in to be with

Alpha. Azril headed out of the worship area with Tom and Murphy behind him. He wanted to greet each disciple as they were on their way out of the housing area to go to the noshery for breakfast.

As he stood by the front doors of the housing area, Azril grabbed his walkie talkie from his pocket in order to communicate with Alpha. "Don't forget about Farrah this morning. She has school duty with Juliet while you are in class with Martin. Hawk and Sparrow will be with Sara. I'm also going to send Samantha in to stay with you as well."

"I gotchu, daddy," Alpha responded.

As he greeted the disciples, several feminine disciples had gathered around him. Since Omegra's passing, Azril would regularly have disciples offering themselves to him as though they wanted to be the leader's next connected partner. He wanted to focus on his children, as well as the disciples within the City of Disciples. He had rejected every offering so far, but Alpha was encouraging him to try and find another connected partner. At that time he wasn't ready to replace Omegra, but he was considering the possibility in the future.

"Good morning, Leader," Pattie said, placing one of her hands on his bicep.

"Good morning, Pattie," he replied.

"It's wonderful to see you today, Leader," Karlie told him.

"It's nice to see you too, Karlie," he responded.

It wasn't long before Stacy, Danielle and Laura joined the others, surrounding him. Becky just walked past him, wiggling her fingers in a flirty wave.

Most of the disciples just walked by with a short, 'good morning' whereas those five feminine disciples seemed to always stop and flirt any time he was among the disciples. He felt as if they were looking for the leader to take them into his housing unit and engage in connected activities.

"Y'all should get going to the noshery before all the food is gone," Azril told them.

Each one of them grazed his torso with their fingertips as they walked away. He wasn't sure how to handle the attention he was receiving, but he also wondered if they were trying to see how far they could go before he either isolated them, or chose one as his next connected partner.

Azril flapped his hand at Tom and Murphy. "Go keep an eye on Jordan and Brad. When you see Samantha, please ask her to come to the office and let her know that the leader is summoning her."

As the last few stragglers headed out, the

leader made his way back to the office to check on Alpha. As he opened the door, Alpha was pulling a few pages off the printer and Martin was sitting in one of the chairs in front of the desk.

"Hi, daddy," Alpha said, turning around.

"Hey, baby girl. How's it going? All of the disciples are out in the noshery. Are you done with the job assignments?" the leader asked.

"Just finished. Are you going to let me hang it up by myself today, or do I still have to be followed around by Martin?" Alpha asked, rolling her eyes.

Azril looked down at his oldest child. "I'm sorry, sweet girl, but you can't go anywhere by yourself. Martin will need to go with you no matter what you are doing."

Alpha sighed heavily. "You know no one has ever tried to harm me because all of the disciples loved mom just as much as we did. I go outside alone, almost daily, to inform Cory of the area where he is to take the disciples to recruit new disciples and everyone treats me with respect."

Azril embraced her. "You know that after what happened to your mother, I'm skeptical of everyone. Cory, Martin and the other disciples guard are always keeping an eye on you when you are out on the property. When you are inside the housing building to post the job assignments, there isn't a single other disciple around. However, when you go out to talk to Cory, there are disciples everywhere. There is more of a chance of potential danger when you are alone. Plus, after what Tom and Murphy has just informed me about, you may be in danger. That is why I have summoned for Samantha to come be with you and Martin. That way, even if you have to go to the bathroom, Martin will be outside waiting and Samantha will be inside with you."

Alpha squeezed her arms around his waist. "I understand, daddy. Mommy was alone when Beatrice and Danny grabbed her and tied her to a tree. How old am I going to be before I start getting my own job assignment?"

"Well, you have advanced so far in your schooling and if you continue on that track, you should be done with school by the time you get to your fifteenth year and you could begin working then. Although, your job assignments would mostly be leader related, rather than disciple related," Azril told her.

"If I'm on track as the successor to the leader of the City of Disciples, then I would like to do the same jobs as all the other disciples. I would like to be able to understand all aspects as to running the City of Disciples. Also, when do I receive the mark of the leader?" Alpha said.

The leader placed his hands on her shoulders and looked down into her eyes. "I can have Martin work with you in understanding the workings of the leader. Cory can take over some days, as he has done my job in my absence. I could also take you around the City of Disciples and you could shadow me someday, I promise. As for the mark of the leader, that will have to wait until your eighteenth year."

"Why can't I get it now?" Alpha whined, as she stomped her foot.

"Because it requires a piece of metal being heated up over an open fire, then that hot piece of metal being pressed into your skin." Azril held out his arm, so his daughter could see the raised scar that signified the mark of the leader.

Alpha traced her fingertips over the mark. "My eighteenth year, you say? I'm okay with that."

She handed Azril the job assignment list in order for him to look it over before it was posted. Just as he handed it back to her, Samantha entered the office. Alpha and Martin headed out to post the job assignments in the disciples common area, as Azril motioned for Samantha to sit in one of the chairs in front of the desk.

The leader sat down in the chair behind the desk and leaned forward against the desk. "I need you to stay with Alpha and Martin today. I have reason to believe that she may be in danger. There isn't any concrete evidence, but since the information has been brought to my attention, I'm not taking it lightly."

Samantha nodded. "Absolutely, Leader. I will keep her safe. She will not be alone at any time, for any reason. You can count on me." She stood and left the office to join Alpha and Martin.

Three

Azril headed back upstairs to make sure that Farrah and Sara had taken his youngest three out to the noshery. The leader was thankful for the disciples guard who take care of his children. Farrah and Sara had been promoted to disciples guard when Omegra had gathered her own twelve disciples guard. Both of them were the only two remaining as disciples guard after Omegra's passing since they had been assigned to the leader's children.

The leader opened the door to his living quarters and saw the two disciples guard trying to wrangle the kids. Juliet was chasing the twins around the common area, as Sara was reaching out to grab the boys and Farrah was reaching for Juliet. Azril whistled loud and the three kids stopped.

"I see you were able to get them dressed for the day, but haven't been able to get them out for breakfast," the leader said.

Sara wrapped her arms around the boys shoulder's, as she knelt down behind them. "I'm sorry leader. Once they were dressed, Juliet decided she wanted to be a monster and chased the boys."

Farrah placed her hands on Juliet's shoulders. "It's my fault. She asked me what would happen if Danny and Beatrice came back and I told her that they would be zombie monsters. That's when she decided to be a zombie monster."

Azril laughed. "I'm so glad that they have chosen to be silly children. Alpha has grown up so fast, I don't think she ever gave herself time to be a child."

They all left the leader's housing quarters and headed to the noshery. Farrah headed over to join

Martin, leaving Juliet with Azril. Alpha was sitting at a table with Samantha and her son, Xavier. The leader, followed by Juliet and the twins, walked over to the table with Alpha.

Sara walked through the food line and grabbed trays for not only the leader's children, but also the leader and herself. She sat down next to the twins, after doling out the food trays.

As they completed their breakfast, Farrah came over to the leader's table. Sara assisted Hawk and Sparrow with cleaning their hands and picking up their food trays, as Farrah assisted Juliet with the same. They directed the kids to take care of their food trays. Sara took the boys to their daily classes, as Farrah hung back to speak with the leader.

"Alpha tells me that I'm on school duty today. Is that just with Juliet, or does that include the other disciples children?" Farrah asked.

"Oh, no. Your only focus is on Juliet. She seems to learn better when you give her one on one attention," Azril told her, as he cuddled his girls.

"You got it, Leader," Farrah said, flashing him a smile.

Farrah took Juliet for her schooling, as Martin and Samantha took Alpha to check on the working disciples before she started her school work.

Once he was completely alone, Pattie, Karlie, Stacy, Danielle, Laura and Becky stepped up to the table the leader was sitting at. He looked up at them, confused as to why they had approached him.

Azril stood. "Shouldn't y'all be at your work assignments?"

"We have something important that we felt needed to be brought to your attention," Pattie said, smiling.

The leader turned and walked out of the noshery heading back toward the housing building, as the feminine disciples followed. "Okay, what is it?"

Karlie stepped in front of him, blocking his path. "Is Alpha suppose to be the one to succeed you as leader?"

Azril tried to take a step forward, but the other five surrounded him. "That's an inappropriate question."

"We are just wondering if Alpha is meant to take over the City of Disciples, or if you would choose one of your masculine heirs," Pattie told him, as she stood behind him, rubbing her hands up his back and over his shoulders.

"This is an extremely inappropriate interaction. Why do y'all feel that it is any of your business who is allocated to take over the City of Disciples?" Azril asked, as the five others stepped closer to him.

All six of them placed one hand on his body and simultaneously recited. "As I stand before the great leader of the City of Disciples, I offer myself to you as a potential connected partner. As I have prepared my womb in order to conceive the next leader of the City of Disciples, I can only focus on the possibility of the honor of a masculine heir. Shall I not succeed, I do hope that I am still worthy of being the connected partner to the leader of the disciples. Please great leader, take my body and fill my womb with your masculine energy and the next leader of the City of Disciples."

The disciples ushered Azril quickly toward the housing building and directly to the office. Pattie forced him to sit on the chair behind his desk, as the six of them removed their tops. "We are here to offer ourselves to the leader."

Azril didn't know what to say at first. "This… this is not the way to offer yourselves to me."

"It has been five years since Omegra passed. You need a connected partner in order to lead the disciples down the right path. It has been so long since you have been able to release some tension and we just want to help you with that," Stacy told him, stepping in front of him and kneeling down between his knees.

"Excuse me? You're not going to help me with

anything," he said, attempting to stand.

Becky raised her eyebrows and pulled her shirt back on. "Fine, but just know that each of us is willing to engage in connected activities with you, should you ever require the release."

The other five followed suit with putting their shirts back on. Stacy rubbed Azril's crotch before they exited the office. The leader took a deep breath, furrowed his brow, trying to process what just happened.

As he rubbed his face with his hands, Samantha entered the office. "Leader, do you have a moment?"

He placed his forearms on his desk in front if him. "As long as you aren't going to ambush me with an offering."

She scrunched up her face, puzzled. "What?"

"Nothing. It has been a strange morning. What can I do for you and why aren't you with Alpha?" Azril asked.

Samantha sat down in one of the chairs in front of the desk. "She's with Martin and Xavier. As you know my son, Xavier, is about the same age as Alpha. He is not excelling as well as I had hoped academically and I know that she is on track to finish her schooling early. I thought it could be beneficial to have the two of them together during class time, but I wanted to run it by you before we made it a regular thing."

Azril reached into his file drawer and pulled out Xavier's school chart. "I know that Alpha had a hard time learning in the group class setting, so Debora allowed her to assist with teaching the other kids, while also completing her own assignments. That was the reason I took her out of the class setting and had her just sit with Martin while she did her assignments. I see here that Debora noted that she believes that Xavier would benefit from some one on one learning. I will ask Alpha if she would be willing to assist him with that. If she agrees, I will have Debora make sure that Martin gets the work for Xavier at the same time he picks up Alpha's classwork."

"Thank you, Leader. I appreciate that," Samantha said, as she stood.

She leaned over the desk and bowed her head. Azril placed his hand on top of her head for blessing, before she turned and left the office. Pattie, Becky, Danielle, Karlie, Stacy and Laura were all waiting in the worship center for Samantha to emerge.

As soon as the door to the office latched closed, Samantha smiled and flashed them a thumbs up. "My son and Alpha will get some alone time. As they get closer, the leader will have no other option than to ensure that Xavier becomes the new leader of the City of Disciples with Alpha at his side."

Pattie curled up one side of her mouth in a sly smile. "Good. Alpha will make a great leader, but we need a masculine heir to succeed the leader. None of the disciples will respect her as much as they have for each one of her parents. That could put you and Lawerence in the leader position if something happens to the leader before Alpha is old enough to take over."

Karlie shook her head. "They would have to convince Cory and Martin that Alpha and Xavier are meant to lead the City of Disciples if anything were to happen to the leader."

Samantha held her hands up in front of her shoulders. "I don't wish harm coming to the leader. I just want Xavier to harness his full potential and lead the new generation of disciples to greatness. He was, after all, the first masculine disciple born within the City of Disciples. The leadership belongs to him."

The six feminine disciples escaped out the side door in the worship area, as the door to the office opened. Samantha had just made it out to the common area when Azril stepped into the worship center. He wanted to meet up with Tom and Murphy to see if they had any new information about the four suspicious disciples. He headed out of the residential building and through the property to locate his disciples guard.

Four

Jordan, Vernon, Gerald and Brad were congregating around the livestock area when Azril was walking the property to interact with the disciples. The leader approached them carefully, trying to catch any part of their conversation.

Gerald stopped their discussion once he noticed Azril approaching. "Good afternoon, Leader. The cows were milked early this morning in order to supply the disciples with a fresh batch for breakfast."

Jordan stood at attention as though he were a disciples guard. "We were also able to get fresh eggs from the chickens. The two pregnant pigs are almost ready to give birth. They can have between seven to twenty piglets each. That means that from the ten we already have, once they give birth, we should be able to slaughter one of the males to feed the disciples."

"That sounds perfect. I'm sure the disciples will appreciate fresh meat. As for the four of you, is there anything I need to know?" Azril asked. The tone in his voice changed between statement and question.

"We are just doing our jobs and trying to live within favor of God from the message as written in the Disciples Doctrine," Brad said, placing his hand on the leader's shoulder.

Azril looked over at Brad's hand, then looked back up at the disciples. "I appreciate that. Unfortunately, there have been some rumblings from the other disciples that the four of you may be thinking about defecting from the City of Disciples. If any of you need to talk, I'm always here to listen. You are also welcome to speak to the disciples guard who is assigned to your tier. Just understand that if any of you do decide to defect and you are caught, you will be placed in isolation with the option of being shunned."

Jordan exchanged glances with the other three. "We can understand your concern, Leader. However, we are just discussing the best ways that we can serve not only God, but also you as the leader of the disciples."

Vernon decided to weigh in on the conversation. "We are thankful for you and everything you have done for us. However, the four of us don't agree with the shunning ceremony. We believe that if a disciple doesn't want to be here, then they should be free to leave."

The leader pushed Brad's hand off his shoulder, then rubbed his forehead. "If the four of you are wanting to live within favor of God from the message as written in the Disciples Doctrine, then you have to accept the shunning ceremony. The shunning ceremony is in the Disciples Doctrine."

Jordan lowered his head and sucked his teeth before looking back up at Azril. "According to the Disciples Doctrine, any outsider or disciple who commits an evil act is to be shunned from the physical land, just as God will shun them from the promised land. In no way does it specify how the outsider or disciple is to be shunned. Couldn't you just kick them out of the City of Disciples without murdering them?"

Azril took one step closer to Jordan. "You are correct. The Disciples Doctrine states that any outsider or disciple who commits an evil act is to be shunned from the physical land. That is not the same as the City of Disciples. The City of Disciples resides on the physical land. That is the specific way that God has told me as to how to shun an outsider or disciple. As well, when the Disciples Doctrine states that God will shun them from the promised land, that means that the one who is shunned will go to the underworld and not the promised land."

Gerald bent his elbows and held his hands up in front of his shoulders as in surrender. "I can understand that you may interpret the message that way, but is it possible that you may have interpreted it wrong?"

The leader took a deep breath and let it out, hard. "First of all, God speaks directly to me during my meditation sessions. He has directed me in the right way to lead the disciples. And secondly, I would never do anything against God and His message."

"That could just be what you believe and not what God has said. It could be interpreted several different ways. Shunning them from the physical land doesn't say to murder them and commit an evil act," Gerald told him, as the other three nodded their heads.

"I am the leader of the disciples. I do not commit evil acts. I enforce God's message," Azril said, through clenched teeth.

Jordan, Vernon, Gerald and Brad didn't know how to respond. The four of them just stood there staring at the leader, as he breathed heavily. After a few seconds, Azril stomped off and approached Tom, who was standing nearby. The leader clasped both hands behind his neck.

"Hey, Leader. I think we should isolate those four disciples. They leave the City of Disciples once a week with the intention of recruiting new disciples, but they never come back with any outsiders. I think they may have been communicating with law enforcement. They have been discussing the shunning ceremony. They find it to be illegal and barbaric," Tom said.

The leader rubbed his face before crossing his arms over his chest. "I think you're right. They all need to spend at least four weeks in isolation. Gerald just accused me of committing evil acts when I shun an outsider or disciple. Alpha has noticed their treason as well. She has decided they will no longer be scheduled to leave for recruiting."

Tom furrowed his brow. "You are the leader of the disciples. God communicated the Disciples

Doctrine to you. That means that you are the only one who doesn't commit evil acts, because you are here on the physical land to enact God's justice."

Azril patted Tom on his back. "Thank you. You are so right. Get the other disciples guard and have them bring those four to me in my office. I will be placing them in isolation. They have no right to speak to me the way they have and due to the fact that they are only conversing with each other, maybe they should be separated for a while."

Five

The leader sat behind the desk after he entered the office. He placed his forearms against his desk laid the palms of his hands flat on top of the surface. He didn't have to wait long for the disciples guard to bring in Jordan, Vernon, Gerald and Brad. He wasn't going to give them a chance to explain their actions.

Azril addressed them as soon as the door to

the office had latched closed. "The four of you have committed an evil act. You have shown disrespect for both God as well as the leader. You are all going to be separated and placed into isolation for the next four weeks."

"Wait, four weeks. We need to go out and recruit new disciples." Jordan stepped closer to the desk.

The leader rose to his feet. "You need to back up! This isn't up for negotiation! Follow me."

Azril led the way to the hatch in the floor. The leader was the first to descend the stairs. Tom nudged Jordan to follow Azril down the stairs. Hesitantly, he took two steps toward the hatch, then turned to face his other co-conspirators. Walter grabbed Vernon's arm, as Tom shoved Jordan.

Jordan stumbled forward. "Okay. I get it."

Tom poked his finger into Jordan's back as he took each step behind him. Walter forced Vernon down the stairs. Murphy pressed his hands against Gerald's back, since he was refusing to move. Last, Warren just crossed his arms over his chest and glared at Brad until he voluntarily descended the stairs. Cory descended the stairs last. The head disciples guard was there as back up.

Azril opened the first four isolation chambers

in order for the disciples to be isolated. Jordan stepped up in front of room one and stopped. He turned and looked at the leader. Azril nodded his head at Tom. Tom shoved Jordan into the room, then slammed the door shut. The leader locked the door to the first isolation chamber, then turned toward the other three. They made the right decision to just enter the next three subsequent rooms and sit on the beds.

"Are you going to visit with them daily for one on one sermons?" Cory asked, as the leader locked the isolation rooms.

Azril pursed his lips. "Absolutely not. They are going to spend the next thirty days locked alone with just their thoughts and the Disciples Doctrine."

"So their meals are just going to be slid in through the peep door at the bottom of each isolation chamber?" Walter asked.

"That's right. I also want to make sure that the audio is working properly down here. If at any point during the next month I hear them trying to communicate with each other, they get more time," Azril said, leading the way up the stairs back to the office.

Cory stayed behind in the isolation area to make sure the surveillance system was completely operable. He went from camera to camera waiving his arms and saying, 'sound test'. Azril would respond back on the walkie talkie with any issues, or let him know that it's good. Luckily, only one camera was having sound issues.

"Thank you, Cory. Get Sean and Joe down there to fix the audio on camera three," the leader requested.

"I have you covered," Cory said over the radio, as he ascended the stairs.

"I appreciate all of you. Each of you have been an asset to not only my disciples guard, but to the disciples here in the City of Disciples. I would like to present all twelve of the disciples guard with a bonus for your loyalty and hard work," Azril announced, after Cory had joined them in the office.

"That's really generous of you. I know we would really all appreciate that. I know a couple of the guys need a few uniforms repaired, or replaced, but they haven't been able to afford the costs," Walter said, presenting his hand to the leader to shake it.

Azril leaned against the front of his desk between the two guest chairs. "Has the price of the uniforms gone up?"

Murphy pursed his lips and nodded his head. "Emma said the price of fabric has gone up, so she had to raise the price of the uniforms. They use to be the price of a week's pay, but now they are a week and a half's pay."

"Is that why it seems like the disciples are requesting to go recruit new disciples, rather than just waiting to be placed on the job assignment list for recruiting?" Azril asked, placing his hands on his knees.

Cory ushered Tom, Walter, Murphy and Warren out of the office, but stayed behind to speak with the leader alone. "Look, ten years ago when we first started gathering the disciples and built the City of Disciples things didn't cost as much as they do now. Cost of living prices have gone up. As a matter of fact, that's one reason why recruitment has been up lately. People have been struggling out there in the world and knowing that they don't have regular bills to pay, or worry that they could be evicted. Unfortunately, within the City of Disciples we are so far removed from the outside world, we have never thought to raise the pay for the disciples."

Azril intertwined his fingers behind his neck, looked up at the ceiling, then made eye contact with his head disciples guard. "At the worship service tonight, I will announce that everyone will be getting a raise. Due to my oversight and lack of knowledge in the outside world I have not done right by the disciples."

Cory stepped up next to Azril and placed his

hand on his shoulder. "I'm sure that everyone within the City of Disciples will appreciate that, Leader."

Azril stood up straight and walked around behind the desk. "Can you send Sharon in here, so I can find out how much I will be able to raise everyone's pay to. She is the one who is assigned to the budget."

"How much are you thinking?" Cory inquired, as he walked over to the door to exit the office.

"If we have enough, I would prefer to double their pay," Azril said.

"I don't think that would be a smart idea. With the rise in living costs, comes the rise in property taxes," Cory told him, as he left the office.

Azril plopped down into his chair behind the desk and rubbed his face. He had never had a real job before, so he wasn't even sure about the right way to pay the disciples. He just hoped that everyone was happy and felt safe in the City of Disciples.

"Leader, Cory said you wanted to see me," Sharon said, as she opened the door to the office about fifteen minutes later.

"Sharon, yes. Please come in. Thank you for coming by so quickly," the leader said, standing.

Sharon closed the door behind her and walked over to sit in one of the chairs in front of the desk.

"I was told to bring the laptop with me, so I have it right here. Whatever you need, just let me know."

The leader explained to Sharon what he wanted. She nodded and got to work formatting a spreadsheet in order to figure out how much they could spare for each disciple. Once she had given him the number, Azril thanked her and began writing out the worship service notes to inform the disciples about the raise, as she left the office to go back to her work assignment.

Six

The worship service erupted into applause when the leader announced that everyone would be getting five more dollars each day and the recruiting bonus would go from two dollars to five. Azril couldn't believe that the City of Disciples had acquired fifty billion dollars.

Emma was making her money from her clothing shop that she had started for the City of Disciples. She not only sold uniforms for the disciples, but she was also selling fashion for the real world. The funds she received from the disciples for their uniforms was what she was able to keep. Sharon helped Emma setup a website for her fashion line. Seventy five percent of her sales was to go to sustain the City of Disciples, whereas twenty five percent went back into her business for supplies.

Sharon was the city's financial advisor, as well as the Disciples Doctrine distributor. She was able to keep all of the funds that came to her from the disciples when they had to purchase the Disciples Doctrine. However, she was also receiving disciple pay for being the city's financial advisor. She made thirty dollars each day for keeping track of the finances.

As the outsiders entered the City of Disciples, once they had relinquished all of their funds to the leader, they would be issued a light blue uniform and given a job assignment within the city. Those new followers were paid two dollars each day for their work. Once they had memorized the evil acts as stated in the Disciples Doctrine, they would be able to participate in God's Cleanse and were then issued a dark blue uniform and given a raise to five dollars per day.

At that point, they would be allowed to leave

the city in order to recruit new outsiders. A bonus of two dollars per outsider they brought in, who were issued light blue uniforms, would be given to every disciple who was able to recruit new followers. Once a disciple had five new recruits that had participated in God's Cleanse, they would be moved up to level one, issued a green uniform and paid ten dollars per day.

In order for a disciple to be promoted into level two, issued an orange uniform and get paid fifteen dollars per day, they would have to have recruited ten new disciples who had participated in God's Cleanse. Level three was paid twenty dollars per day, issued a red uniform and had recruited fifteen new disciples who had participated in God's Cleanse. The top level, level four, was paid twenty five dollars per day, issued a brown uniform and had recruited twenty new disciples who had participated in God's Cleanse.

The disciples guard all wore grey uniforms and were paid thirty dollars per day. As for the disciples children, they were only allowed a yellow uniform until their fifteenth year when it would be traded for the light blue uniform and they would go through all the same steps as the new disciples. Adding the extra five dollars per day for each disciple was accommodating since all of their needs were being met within the City of Disciples.

"I understand the price of uniforms have gone up, as well as the price of the Disciples Doctrine. Parents are having to purchase extra copies of the Disciples Doctrine for their children when they reach their tenth year. The rising cost of groceries has caused the meal prices at the noshery to go up and I was informed that some of the single disciples were skipping meals. Breakfast is free due to the fact that the ingredients are grown right here in the City of Disciples. Does anyone have any other ideas for the disciples to make more money?" the leader asked, allowing the disciples to chime in.

Nurse Gayle was the first to stand up. "I would like to suggest that instead of the City of Disciples paying for the medical care of the disciples, maybe the disciples could pay for individualized medical care."

"That's interesting. Tell me what you're thinking, Gayle," Azril inquired.

Gayle smiled. "This is my thought, Doctor Kyle and I are being paid the same daily rate as level four. That includes when we don't have any patients. I feel like we should set appointments for the disciples to come get regular check ups rather than them only showing up when there is an emergency."

The leader nodded. "I see where you are going

with that. You think that you can keep the disciples healthy if you have them come in regularly. Is there a specific amount you would charge that wouldn't cause the disciples to never seek medical care?"

"Two dollars for a check up, five for emergency care and ten per trimester of pregnancy. Any specialty care pricing will depend on how many times they have to come in for monitoring," Gayle informed.

"That sounds like a great idea. Let's take a vote with the disciples. Cory and Walter will be coming around to collect the voting sheets. Write yes if you agree with Nurse Gayle, or no if you want the City of Disciples to continue paying for the healthcare that most of you don't take advantage of," Azril stated.

Every disciple reached into the pocket of the pew in front of them, retrieved a small piece of paper and a golf pencil to vote on the medical care. Some of them discussed the situation before voting and others seemed to be writing more than just the one word response.

As the two head disciples guard wandered through the worship area, the leader stood at the podium and looked out over all the disciples. Some were smiling, where others seemed to look stressed. Azril didn't want the disciples to feel stressed.

"While Cory and Walter tally up the votes, I would like to hear from the other disciples who may have any other ideas," the leader suggested.

One disciple suggested they sell some of their fresh produce, as well as the eggs. Azril didn't realize that they were producing so many fresh fruits and vegetables that more of them were going bad before they could be consumed. The leader didn't even take a vote for that, he just agreed.

When Cory brought out the tally about the medical care, the leader was shocked that all the disciples agreed to pay for their own doctor visits. Some of them even explained why it was a great idea.

Seven

The four disciples in isolation had spent six days of silent reflection. Everything in the City of Disciples seemed to be running smoothly with them being in isolation. The atmosphere throughout the entire property was relaxed and every job assignment was running like a well oiled machine.

"How is it that we continue to recruit disciples that cause such chaos throughout the entirety of the City of Disciples?" Azril asked Cory, as they sat in a golf cart and looked out at the working disciples.

Cory started the golf cart and drove around the property. "They seem like they genuinely want to be here at first. Then they act like they know how to lead the disciples better than you. However, Jordan, Vernon, Gerald and Brad seem to be working further than that of Beatrice and Danny."

Azril looked over at Cory. "How so?"

Cory drove the golf cart to the far back of the property, where Omegra had been found tied to a tree. He stopped, turned in his seat to face the leader. "Beatrice and Danny seemed to think if they could hurt you and eliminate your connected partner, they would be able to take over the City of Disciples. The four disciples in isolation have been holding secret meetings outside the city's walls, as if they are figuring out a way to take down the entire city. The difference is, the two that were shunned wanted to lead the disciples, the four in isolation want to disband the disciples."

The leader took a deep breath and looked through the trees, as if he could see the ghost of his connected partner. "I'm tired of feeling as though I'm being challenged for the role of the leader of the City of Disciples when I'm the one that God gave His message to."

Cory started up the golf cart and drove back through the property. As the two of them rounded the front of the property near the gate, they could hear voices on the other side. The two disciples guard at the front gates were pressed against it as if they were trying to hear what was happening on the other side. The gate was made of thick oak, ten feet high, two doors that were ten feet wide each that opened vertically in the center, had a ten foot long wooden bar slid into the metal handles on each door in order to keep the outsiders out.

Cory stopped the cart and the two of them approached the gate. "Tom, Murphy, what is going on?"

Tom stepped away from the gate and approached the leader and Cory. "We don't know what's going on, but it has been going on for over an hour."

Azril rubbed his forehead. "This has been going on for over an hour and you didn't think to assemble all of the guards?"

"We haven't even opened the spy window. We have just been listening to more and more outsiders gather on the other side," Murphy told them.

"Open the spy window," Cory said, as he

walked up to the gate.

Murphy slid the pin hatch open, Tom led Azril over to the side wall so he wasn't standing in front of the gate while Cory looked through the spy window. The head disciples guard took a few minutes to take in everything that was transpiring outside of the City of Disciples before he stepped back.

"There is an entire SWAT team that has assembled out there," Cory told the leader.

"Why is there a SWAT team outside of the City of Disciples?" Azril said, linking his hands behind his neck.

Cory pulled the walkie talkie out of his pocket. "Attention all disciples guard. We have a stage three threat at the front gate that could potentially turn into a stage four at any moment. Everyone needs to assemble at the front gate, immediately."

"Murphy, sound the alarm. We may need to go down to the stock room armory. I'm the leader of the disciples and I have promised to keep everyone here in the City of Disciples safe. If they storm the property, we have all rights to protect the city and the disciples in it," Azril said, as he climbed onto the golf cart.

Murphy cranked the alarm that sounded over the entire City of Disciples. It wailed out like a tornado siren. Azril drove the cart around the property to make sure the disciples were getting into position for an emergency.

The feminine disciples gathered the children and headed up the side entrance to the leader's living quarters, as the masculine disciples headed inside the housing building to wait for the order to go down to the stock armory.

Once all of the disciples guard had arrived at the gate, Cory gave them a run down of the situation on the other side. "At this point we are unarmed and unprepared for what may transpire. We need to head to the armory and wait for the leader's order." The disciples guard all agreed and hurried through the property toward the housing building after they reinforced the entrance.

Azril stood on top of the stock hatch surrounded by the disciples. "The SWAT team is outside the City of Disciples. That could only mean one thing; a disciple has betrayed us. Before we arm ourselves, I need someone to tell me who it was right now."

As the disciples guard entered the housing building, Lawerence raised his hand. "I have a feeling I know who it was. The four of them are down in isolation."

"Are you telling me that Jordan, Vernon, Gerald and Brad are the disciples who betrayed us?" the leader asked.

Lawerence nodded. "It's a theory, but I believe the four of them have something to do with what is happening right now. Since they have been leaving the City of Disciples for recruiting, but never coming back with any outsiders for the past year or so. As of this moment, the SWAT team is trying to break down the front gate and we need to arm ourselves."

Azril sighed heavily, then opened the hatch to the stock room. Cory led the way down the stairs as the disciples created a line from the armory lockup up the stairs and into the common area. Guns were shuffled down the line until everyone was in possession of an AR-15.

Eight

Azril led the disciples out of the housing building. "Everyone take their posts. If you need any direction, please ask the disciples guard at the head of your tier."

Cory took the lead with directing the disciples. "Tier one through six on the right, seven through twelve on the left. Any disciples on the front line will be laying on the ground and be the first to fire.

The disciples behind them will be on their knees and will cover the front line. Everyone else after that will stand in a checkered formation. If a disciple is standing in front of you, you are to hold your fire until that disciple goes down. Is everyone ready to be released into the promised land if it were to be God's will?"

"LET'S GO!" every disciple yelled in unison.

As the banging on the front gate began splintering the railroad ties holding the entrance closed, the disciples took formation. The disciples guard stood at the back of the disciples with Azril behind them.

When the railroad ties finally split and the front gate flew open, the police and SWAT stood outside the perimeter. No one fired their guns, as the disciples were informed to only return fire if fired upon.

From the outside of the gate, a voice from a bullhorn bellowed through the City of Disciples. "We are here to speak with the leader. There are four police officers that entered your group and they haven't checked in in over a week. Just send them out and surrender, or we will be forced to storm the grounds."

"Cory, take Walter to the entrance and talk to the police. I'm going to take Martin, Tom and Murphy to go down to the isolation chambers to retrieve the defectors," Azril instructed.

The leader and the three disciples guard walked into the housing building, as Cory and Walter headed up to the entrance. The two head disciples guard aimed their guns at the line of SWAT that stood in front of the gates as they approached.

"Please put down your weapons," one guy in a SWAT uniform ordered, pointing his gun at them.

Cory and Walter held their stance, as Cory continued the conversation. "The leader is willing to release the isolated defectors, but the disciples will not be surrendering."

"We will be forced to take fire if you refuse to surrender," the SWAT guy explained.

Walter took a step back. "There are thousands of disciples prepared to fire back. The leader has promised every disciple protection and safety within the City of Disciples and you are compromising our safety. We will do everything to protect ourselves."

The voice from the bullhorn boomed over the line of SWAT in front of the head disciples guard. "We have reason to believe that your leader has murdered over one hundred people. Not only that, but apparently several of your so called disciples are being held against their will and there are children in danger."

Cory stepped back to stand next to Walter. "All disciples are free to leave whenever they want and absolutely NONE of the children are in danger."

The bullhorn voice returned a response. "If that's true, to any disciples who would like to leave on their own recognizance, please do so now."

Cory and Walter retreated back to the line of disciples guard. Everyone waited for a disciple to move toward the exit. Lawerence heard shuffling in the wooded area behind them and moved in line to approach Cory.

"I think there is someone moving within the trees," Lawerence told the head disciples guard.

"Do you know who it is?" Cory asked.

Lawerence shook his head. "I can't see anyone, but I know I heard movement."

Cory jerked his head to the side. "Go check it out. It could just be an animal, but there could also be defectors."

"What do I do if it is disciples?" Lawerence wondered.

"We will allow the leader to decide if they are going into isolation, or an execution style shunning," Cory told him.

Lawerence slowly stepped toward the wooded area of the property. He snuck between the trees and found Farrah and Samantha leading some children and their mothers along the property line toward the exit.

Lawerence approached Farrah. "What are y'all doing?"

Samantha pushed Xavier and Alpha behind her. "If y'all are about to start a shoot out, we are going to save the children."

"You know the children would be safer inside the leader's quarters. Turn back now, or face the consequences," Lawerence told them, aiming the AR-15 at Juliet.

Farrah stepped in front of Juliet. "I can't believe you would aim your gun at the leader's child."

Lawerence looked through all of the children they had with them. "Speaking of the leader's children, where are Hawk and Sparrow?"

"They insisted on staying to protect the City of Disciples, so they are still in the leader's quarters with Sara, Sharon and Emma," Samantha told him.

"I wanted to stay too, but I wanted Xavier to stay with me. His mother told him it wasn't safe, so I chose to go with Xavier instead," Alpha said.

"Turn back, or the disciples guard could turn around and just begin firing into the woods thinking it is a cop trying to sneak into the property,"

Lawerence warned.

Samantha slapped her thigh. "Lawerence, just let us go. You could come with us. Xavier is your son too. Let's get out of here before anyone starts dying."

"That's another reason I want you to go back. I have a plan. If any gunfire is exchanged, I will come get you and I know a safer way off the property. Now go back," Lawerence said, embracing his connected partner.

Farrah and Samantha shot glances at each other, nodded and turned, guiding the children back toward the leader's quarters. When Lawerence reemerged from the wooded area, he lied and told Cory it was just a family of deer.

Nine

Azril exited the housing building holding one end of a rope. Jordan, Vernon, Gerald and Brad had that same rope tied around their waists. The leader was guiding them out, through the property like cattle. Martin, Tom and Murphy followed behind, as they all walked toward the front gate.

"This is not a negotiation. I'm willing to hand over these four traitors, but none of the disciples will be leaving here. We are the disciples of God and we will appease Him in worship," Azril told the police, as he stopped at the entrance to the city.

"We are the disciples of God and we will appease Him in worship," every gun toting disciple echoed.

Martin, Tom and Murphy poked the four prisoners in their backs with their AR-15s and forced them out toward the SWAT. Azril dropped the end of the rope he was holding and allowed Jordan, Vernon, Gerald and Brad to leave the city.

Once the four undercover officers had made it through the gate, the leader motioned for the three disciples guard to close the gate. All the disciples held their positions as Azril helped to reinforce and lock the entrance.

The voice over the bullhorn screeched. "We are prepared to storm the property if you don't release everyone inside. The leader of this compound is under arrest."

Cory waited for Azril to return to the line. "What do you want us to do, Leader?"

Azril shook his head, then walked up to the front line of disciples and addressed everyone. "As you all know, the mission of the City of Disciples is acceptance, tolerance and equality. You all came here for a reason, then you stayed. I have done everything I could to keep each and every one of you safe. I have matched some of you with your connected partners and I have blessed all of your children after they were born. All I ask of you is to help me protect the City of Disciples. This is our city. Now, do you stand with me as your leader, or do you want to surrender to the outsiders?"

The leader waited for any disciples to make their move. Slowly, several disciples placed their guns on the ground and stepped forward, approaching the leader.

Luke reached out to shake Azril's hand. "I really appreciate everything you have done for me here. Thank you for the opportunity to be a disciple and live in the City of Disciples. Thank you for making me feel important and safe. However, we can't compete with the outsider's law enforcement. I'm sorry."

Azril shook Luke's hand, raised the AR-15 he was holding, aiming it directly at the disciple's chest and pulled the trigger. Luke's body dropped to the ground as the sound of the gun shot echoed over the city. The fifty or so other disciples who were planning to defect with Luke, all bent their elbows and held their hands up in front of their shoulders.

The leader turned his attention to the other defectors and pulled the trigger, firing the AR-15 into the flesh of each one of them. They all dropped to the ground, staining the foliage crimson as they all bled out.

Azril slowly lowered his weapon, as he glared at the dead traitors. He looked up at the rest of the disciples ready with their guns. Each one of them nodded at him, as they silently gave him their approval. He nodded back, turned, then slowly walked toward the housing building and opened the door. He turned his head, looking at the disciples over his shoulder and yelled, "FIRE!"

Ten

The front line of disciples emptied the one hundred round magazines in their guns through the front gate of the City of Disciples. The SWAT team returned fire and the rest of the disciples joined in.

As the sound of gun shots rang out through the City of Disciples, Azril ran up the stairs to the leader's living quarters. A loud explosion sounded from somewhere out on the property, as he stepped up to the door, causing the building to shake. Lawerence appeared from the other staircase and they both pressed their arms against the walls in order to steady their footing.

"What are you doing?" Azril asked his disciples guard.

Lawerence pointed at the door. "I was going to try and save the feminine disciples and the children."

The leader nodded his head. "Me too. I want to get my children out of here safely. That includes Farrah, Sara and Samantha."

"Let's go. I have a secret path to the neighboring property for this specific reason. I have also conspired with Cory and Martin, so they are waiting for us on the pathway," Lawerence informed him.

Azril opened the door and found everyone huddled in the common area. Most of the children were crying and the feminine disciples were doing their best to comfort them.

Alpha ran up to Azril and wrapped her arms around his waist. "What is going on out there?"

"Alpha, where are your siblings?" the leader asked, placing his hands on her shoulders and pushing her away from him.

His oldest daughter pointed toward the kitchenette area. "Juliet is hiding under the sink, Hawk and Sparrow are just in the cabinets."

Lawerence began ushering everyone out and down the side staircase. Azril and Alpha went over to get Juliet, Hawk and Sparrow out of the cabinets.

"Are we going to die?" Hawk asked, as he climbed out of the cabinet.

"No, we are going to get out of here. Come on," Azril told him.

"Why is there so many gun shots?" Sparrow wondered.

The leader embraced his children. "We are under attack. We need to get out of here now."

Azril took his children out of the leader's living quarters and rushed them to the side staircase. They began descending the stairs, just as they heard footsteps coming up from the staircase that led to the office.

The leader didn't want to wait for his daughter to slowly and carefully descend the steps, so he scooped Alpha up into his arms in order to rush down the stairs. "You really need to get over your fear of stairs. I don't understand what you're afraid of."

Alpha felt as though the leader was scolding her. She squirmed and wiggled to get out of his arms the second his feet touched the level ground. "Put me down."

Once she was out of his arms, Alpha ran to catch up with the rest of the disciples, but mostly for Xavier. Azril slowly walked behind, as his three youngest children raced to fall in line.

"Freeze!" a voice shouted from behind the leader.

He turned around to see five SWAT officers in full riot gear standing behind him, aiming M-16 guns at him. Azril crossed his arms over his chest and pursed his lips.

"Don't move! Azril Zion, you're under arrest," an officer behind the SWAT line said.

"You have the wrong guy. I'm Jerry. The leader stayed with his disciples. I was trying to escape with the others," Azril lied.

The five SWAT officers turned around and looked at the police officer behind them. When they started chattering over whether or not they had the right guy, Azril sprinted toward the escaping disciples.

"Hurry up! They are right behind you!" Lawerence shouted.

Azril made it to the secret path, just as a bullet sliced through his shoulder. He stumbled toward his disciples guard who helped him slipped into the neighboring property. Martin, Cory and Lawerence covered the path to block the officers.

"Head to the back of the property. There is a wildlife preserve on the other side that is heavily wooded and I have set up a temporary mini City of Disciples in there," Lawerence told him.

"I think I'm going to bleed out," Azril said, as blood ran down his arm and dripped off his finger tips.

"Doctor Kyle came with us. He's back there with the children. We need to hurry before they get through," Lawerence told the leader, helping him walk as the color drained from Azril's face.

Eleven

By the time Lawerence made it to the nature preserve with all the others, he was carrying Azril. The leader had passed out from the blood loss. He set Azril down on the ground in front of Kyle and cut his shirt off down his injured arm.

"What the fuck do we do now?" Cora asked, tears streaming down her face.

Sara scowled and grabbed Cora's arm. "There

are children here and just because the leader is out of commission for the time being doesn't mean you need to use profanity!"

Sharon wrapped her arms around Cora, trying to comfort her. "The leader will be fine. Kyle will take care of him, then he will take care of us."

"Cora, you need to acknowledge that your words are inappropriate around the children," Sara pressed.

"Fine, Sara. I'm sorry for what I said in front of the children, but I'm scared," Cora cried.

"He got lucky because it was a through and through, but he has lost a lot of blood. When the sun goes down, Gayle and I will sneak back over to the City of Disciples for a few supplies. He needs a blood transfusion," Kyle said, as he bandaged the leader's wound.

Debora cuddled into Cory's arms. "Do you know what happened to the rest of the disciples?"

Cory kissed his connected partner on top of her head. "Martin and I were able to get away just as the SWAT team blew open the gate and began executing everyone."

"At least the gun shots stopped," Alpha said, as she sat on the ground next to Azril with her siblings.

"It was scary. All those guys in their black outfits carrying the walls with the peep window. I thought they were going to kill us," Juliet said.

Alpha cocked her head to the side. "What do you mean the walls with the peep window?"

Juliet held her hands up to her face. She touched the tips of her thumbs together and placed them across her nose, with her fingers straight up next to her eyes. "The walls they had to block themselves from getting hit with bullets."

Xavier smiled at Alpha. "I think she means the SWAT guys with their riot shields."

Martin held his hands up. "Look, we are going to have to keep moving. We can only hide out here for so long before the police find us. Is anyone willing to help me create a stretcher, so we can carry the leader until he recovers?"

"I'll help you," Cory offered.

"Count me in," Lawerence agreed.

"I have one of those at the medical center in the City of Disciples that I can bring back with me when I go back for supplies," Kyle told them.

Cory slowly nodded, then motioned for Martin and Lawerence to join him behind a group of trees. "We will need to make that stretcher. The SWAT team bombed the medical center. The only medical supplies we have here is all that is left."

Martin pointed at Cory. "Yes, we can never go back to the City of Disciples. The entire property has been taken over by the police and by the time they find all the bodies in the shunning pit, we will all be on the most wanted list."

Lawerence placed his right hand on Martin's shoulder. "I have a plan for that. We tell them that we had to follow the leader due to the threat of shunning. Not only that, but if he doesn't make it, it could be easier to get us out of this."

"The two of you sound like defectors. Y'all are a part of the disciples guard. That means the leader chose you because y'all were loyal to the disciples and the message of God as written in the Disciples Doctrine," Cory scolded.

"Oh, give it up. The entire City of Disciples was swarmed by the police. We no longer have to refer to Azril as the leader. It was nice while it lasted, but Cory, it's over now and we all have to go back to the real world," Lawerence told him.

Cory took a deep breath and let it out, loudly. "Look, when the leader denounces his position, or is released into the promised land, then I will stop referring to him that way. At this point, he is at the least our friend and he needs our help."

Martin nodded and began gathering supplies to create the stretcher. "I can't believe that most of the disciples are dead."

"I can't believe how dumb those SWAT officers were," Alpha said, appearing from between two trees.

"What do you mean by that?" Cory asked her.

Alpha bent down and picked up a stick. "Dad was stopped by four SWAT officers and a police officer in a suit. When the police officer said that Azril Zion was under arrest, dad told them he was Jerry and the leader was with his disciples. The SWAT officers turned around to ask the police officer if they had the right guy and that was all the time he needed to run."

"Isn't that the reason they shot him? Because he ran?" Lawerence asked.

Alpha shrugged. "It was either because he ran, or because when they turned toward the officer he confirmed he was who they were looking for."

Lawerence patted her on top of her head. "How is he doing?"

"Doctor Kyle was able to stop the bleeding, but he's worried that dad lost too much and he may not wake up. Juliet, Hawk and Sparrow are with him right now. Farrah, Sara, Katie and Samantha have bags of food that should sustain us for a few days, but if we could get into the food storage bunker, we should be able to get enough food to sustain us for months. Although, there is the possibility that the fifty duffle bags Sharon wheeled over here in the wagon contain all of the funds from the City of Disciples," Alpha said, snapping twigs into small pieces.

Cory placed his hand on her shoulder and looked down at her. "We are going to do everything we can to help your dad. Right now we are trying to gather material to help transport him."

Alpha hugged Cory around his waist, resting her head on his stomach and cried. "The three of you are loyal disciples and I appreciate you."

Lawerence knelt down next to Alpha. "Why don't you go over with your siblings and be with your dad."

The leader's eldest daughter nodded, then disappeared back through the trees. Once he was sure she couldn't hear him, Cory smiled at the other two disciples guards and drummed the tips of his fingers together. "If Sharon was able to recover all of the funds from the City of Disciples, that means we have billions and there would be no reason for us to go back into the city."

Twelve

Alpha was gathering pine needles, leaves and trying to find the right sized branches that would be strong enough to transport the leader. Cory, Martin and Lawerence emerged out from the trees and assisted Alpha. Once they had gathered more than they actually needed, they carried everything they had back over where the rest of the surviving disciples were.

Cory laid the branches down on the ground and tied pine needles together. Martin, Lawerence and Alpha watched him for a while with their heads tilted to the side.

Once Cory started covering the pine needles with the leaves they collected, Lawerence had to speak up. "Hey guy, do you think that is strong enough to hold Azril?"

"The pine needles are like twine and the leaves are to give it the illusion of a backboard," Cory said, shrugging.

Alpha giggled. "We can use the branches, but the rest of that isn't strong enough to carry a newborn baby."

"How about you get on it and we will find out exactly how strong it is," Cory told her, putting his fists on his hips.

Alpha shrugged, then laid down between the branches. Cory stood at her feet, as Lawerence stood at her head. On the count of three, the disciples guard grabbed each end and lifted. Alpha remained on the ground, as the pine needles broke and the branches were the only thing they were able to lift.

Cory lowered his head. "Okay Alpha, you seem to be the academic genius. Do you have a better idea?"

"As a matter of fact, I do," Alpha said, as she

walked away.

"Where is she going?" Cory asked.

"Give her a minute. I have seen her create something new from ordinary objects," Martin told them.

Cory crossed his arms over his chest. After a few minutes, Alpha returned with a sleeping bag and a spool of twine. She opened the sleeping bag and laid it out flat, then placed one branch in the center before folding it over. The second branch was placed at the zipper opening. She used the twine to reinforce the branches.

Alpha tied off the twine, then laid down on the sleeping bag. "Now lift me up."

Cory and Lawerence took the same places as before and lifted the branches. Not only were they able to lift the branches, but they were also able to lift Alpha that time. They placed her back down on the ground.

Martin clapped his hands. "I told you she could do it."

Cory laughed. "I can't believe I was bested by an eight year old."

Alpha bounced up to her feet. "Just think of it this way, I'm the brains and you're the brawn."

"You know what, I'll take it," Cory said, giving Alpha a high five.

"Technically, while my dad is recovering, I'm

the leader of disciples and you are my disciples guard," Alpha said, crossing her arms over her chest and smiling.

"Oh peanut, technically I'm your disciples guard and these two guys are just peons," Martin told her.

Alpha and Martin laughed together then gave each other a high five and a low five. The two of them left Cory and Lawerence behind with their mouths open.

"How's he doing, Doc?" Alpha asked, as they approached the area where Azril was laying on the ground.

"Alpha, I think you need to come over here with your siblings," Doctor Kyle told her.

Juliet had curled up next to Azril. She had wrapped his arm around her. Hawk and Sparrow were sitting next to Azril on his other side. They had pulled his arm up and laid it across their laps. All three of the children were crying.

Alpha dropped her shoulders and slouched. "What is going on?"

Kyle stood up and walked over to Alpha. "The leader's pulse is weak and if I can't get back to the medical center to get what I need to do a blood transfusion, he won't make it much longer."

"Juliet, get up and come with me. We will sneak onto the property and get what Kyle needs," Alpha told her sister.

"You can't do that. The police probably already have child services over there to take you," Martin warned her.

Alpha reached down and forced her sister to stand up. "No! I know how to get onto the property and get to the medical center without being noticed. I have been sneaking out here for the past two years without anyone noticing."

Martin rubbed his forehead. "I noticed, Alpha. I have been assigned as your private disciples guard for five years. I always know where you are at all times. Even when you thought no one is watching."

"Damn it!" Alpha screamed, allowing Juliet to return to her position next to Azril.

"Can't daddy just grow more blood?" Sparrow asked.

"No, stupid. People don't grow blood," Alpha said, sitting down next to Azril's head.

"You're mean," Hawk told Alpha, hugging his brother.

Alpha kissed her dad on his forehead, then leaned toward his ear and whispered. "You can't leave us behind. Me, Juliet, Hawk and Sparrow all need you."

Azril's eyes suddenly fluttered open. Alpha tapped Juliet on top of her head and she sat up.

Martin sat down next to the boys and Kyle rushed over in order to take the leader's vital signs.

Thirteen

Azril slowly lifted his hand and gently touched Juliet's face. "My sweet girls. Alpha, I need you to take care of your brothers. Martin, I want you and Farrah to take my children and give them a good home. Alpha is meant for great things, make sure you allow her to spread her wings."

"What is happening?" Alpha asked.

"I'm not going to make it. Alpha you are meant

to be a leader. Lead your brothers and sister and guide them down the right life plan from the Disciples Doctrine. Remember your roots and the message as told to me from God," Azril said, before his eyes closed and he took his last breath.

Kyle stuck his stethoscope ear pieces into his ears. With his forefinger on the bell and the diaphragm on Azril's chest, the doctor listened for the leader's heartbeat. "He's gone."

All four of the leader's children cuddled with his body and mourned. Kyle, Gayle, Martin and Lawerence stepped away allowing the children to have a moment alone with their dad.

Lawerence sat down next to Samantha and wrapped his arms around her shoulders. "I wonder if we would be able to bury the leader next to Omegra in the City of Disciples."

Samantha rested her head on her connected partner's shoulder. "That would be really nice if we could. I think the kids would like that."

Alpha stood up, wiped the tears from her face and forced the other children to their feet as well. "I'm in charge now. We are going to live off the land, just like dad did when he was a kid."

Juliet pushed her fists into her hips. "I thought you wanted to be Xavier's connected partner."

Alpha sighed heavily. "We can bring him with us. Without mom and dad, it's just us kids leading the disciples. As soon as the police clear out of the City of Disciples, we will move in again."

"No! Daddy said we are 'posed to go with Martin and Farrah and that's where I'm going," Hawk said.

"Me too," Sparrow agreed.

The twins walked away to join the other disciples. Alpha stomped her foot. "Y'all can't leave! I'm in charge now!"

"Dad was in his thirteenth year before he went out on his own. Alpha, we need to stay with Martin and Farrah for a while," Juliet told her older sister.

"Forget it. Just leave me alone," Alpha told Juliet, turning away from her.

"I have a few questions," Martin said.

"I have a plan. What do you want to know?" Lawerence asked.

Martin stood up. "Are we staying here tonight? And where do we go from here?"

Lawerence nodded. "I can understand your concern."

"Also, what do we do about the leader?" Cory asked.

Alpha walked up with tears streaming down her face. "He's dead. He should be buried next to my mother."

Xavier stepped over next to Alpha and hugged

her. "If you want to stay with us for a little while, I know my mother would be okay with that."

"I wanna go ever Alpha goes," Hawk said.

"We are suppose to go with Martin and Farrah. I'm staying with them," Juliet said, cuddled into Farrah's arms.

Alpha rubbed her face on Xavier's shirt. "Dad's last declaration was that the four of us were to go with Martin and Farrah. Right now we need to find a place to live. There is no way that we can stay in the woods. Hawk and Sparrow turn five tomorrow and I had a party planned for them. Juliet will be seven soon and then I will be nine. We need a stable home environment."

Lawerence nodded. "She's right. We need to pool all the money we have together and find homes for all of us."

Sharon held up one of the many duffle bags that were sitting in the wagon. "I actually brought all the bags of money from the City of Disciples with us. We have billions to share between us all."

Lawerence held his hands up. "New plan. We stay here for the night. Sneak into the City of Dis-ciples and drop the leader off next to Omegra, then go find a place to live. There are more chil-dren than we have parents, so we are going to have to split up the children as well."

Cory stood up. "Maybe we could purchase a

building that could accommodate everyone. That way, we don't have to figure out who has to go where and we can continue worshiping God from the message as written in the Disciples Doctrine. These children only know the message from the Disciples Doctrine and that message is the most positive."

Debora stood next to her connected partner. "I agree with Cory. We can stay here for the night, but tomorrow we need to find a permanent home."

Katie and Cora began preparing food for the somewhere around fifty disciples and children that had escaped the City of Disciples. They were able to smuggle out enough food for at least a week. Luckily, since Sharon was able to get all of the funds from the city, they should be able to sustain everyone for several years.

After dinner, Juliet snuggled back in with Azril on one side, as the twins snuggled in on the other side. Alpha laid down above his head, with Xavier curled up behind her. Some of the disciples set up tents to sleep in, whereas others just found a spot on the ground to hunker down for the night.

Fourteen

The next morning, Katie and Cora had set up a fire pit with a grill grate over top in order to prepare breakfast for everyone, while Cory, Martin, Lawerence and Kyle put Azril on the makeshift stretcher. Alpha gathered Juliet, Xavier and the twins and took them into a secluded area away from the others.

"I have a plan. Look, the disciples guard believes that the police are still on the property. When we take dad over to be with mom, if the police are there, they will swarm us. We should run and live on our own. I'm not going to go to live with anyone who's not a disciple. Sharon will most likely not take the money, so when we run, we will come back here and grab the wagon," Alpha began.

"What about transportation? Shouldn't we take one of the golf carts?" Xavier asked.

Alpha pointed at him. "That's good. It might take a couple of days before we will be able to accomplish that, so we will need to hang out around here for a while."

Juliet raised her hand. "Would we be able to get more food and can we bring Farrah with us? We need someone to cook."

"I have been assigned to meal duty a ton of times, so I know how to cook. I can teach everyone how to be self-sufficient. There are things that dad trained me to do that you don't know about. I was going to take over the City of Disciples and know how to do this. Just trust me," Alpha said, stomping her foot on the ground.

Xavier hugged Alpha. "This sounds like a 'Lord of the Flys' situation, but I love it. We can do this."

Alpha pulled away from Xavier. "This is a last resort kind of situation. Right now everything is fine. This plan is only if things go south."

"Are you kids going to join us?" Farrah asked, peeking through the trees.

"We need you in this deal," Juliet said, pulling Farrah into the plan.

Farrah rubbed her face. "I don't think the five of you are capable of taking care of yourselves. How about we all hang back and if things go south, I can take care of you."

Alpha stomped her foot again. "Dang it, Juliet. That's not how this was suppose to go. I'm the leader of the disciples now and I refuse to take orders from the babysitter."

"I'm a grown up. I have legal rights in the outside world to purchase a house that we can all live in, so none of you have to live like hobos in the woods," Farrah told her.

Alpha crossed her arms over her chest. "Whatever. I knew I shouldn't have told Juliet. She's not ready to be on her own."

Farrah guided the children back through the trees. "Let's just go have breakfast."

Xavier held back with Alpha, as Farrah led Juliet, Hawk and Sparrow to where the other disciples were. He cupped her face in his hands and gazed into her eyes.

"If we can't get them on board, then the two of us should do this alone," Xavier told her.

"I know your mother was trying to put us together so I could be your connected partner when we grew to our eighteenth year, but I had already decided that God was the one who brought us together," Alpha told him.

"Let's go. Don't let on that we still have a plan," Xavier told her.

Alpha nodded and they walked hand in hand back to the area where the disciples were having breakfast. None of the disciples were talking, or eating. They all sat with their plates and looked at Alpha.

The leader's oldest daughter looked around at everyone. "Why is everyone staring at me?"

Martin stepped up next to her and whispered in her ear. "The disciples are waiting for you to recite the before meal prayer."

"Oh," Alpha said. "Before we receive these gifts you have provided for us, God, we thank you for the physical land and all the crops, flocks and herds that you have maintained for us in order to nourish our bodies. We are Disciples of God and we will appease You in worship."

"We are Disciples of God and we will appease You in worship," the disciples repeated.

Everyone ate breakfast in silence. Since it was the morning of Azril's release ceremony, the disciples were mourning. The only sound that the disciples should make on the day of another disciples release ceremony is for prayer. Sadness could be felt from everyone.

Fifteen

Before the disciples all gathered to return the leader to the City of Disciples, Alpha was expected to lead the release ceremony. The disciples gathered around Azril's feet, as she took position at his head.

Alpha held her arms out, with the palms of her hands facing the promised land just as Azril always had. "Today we are here as our beloved leader has been released into the promised land. The leader allowed God into his heart in order to share the message with the disciples through the Disciples Doctrine. Since he was a loyal follower of God, he will be welcomed into the promised land just as God has told us about.

"As he reunites with his connected partner, we worship God and await for our release day. God will give us the strength to continue to follow Him as well as giving us the understanding as to why the leader was chosen to leave the physical land to be released into the promised land.

"If anyone has any memories of the leader they would like to share, please feel free to come up here and let us know all the good memories you have." Alpha walked over and sat down next to Juliet.

Cory was the first to step up. "I have been the leader's head disciples guard from the beginning. That's ten years of being by his side. He was my mentor and my confidant. He will be missed, but I am confident that his daughter Alpha, will have no problem filling his shoes in the leader role."

Martin and Farrah both stepped up together. Martin started. "The main message in the Disciples Doctrine is tolerance, equality and acceptance. When I told the leader that I was a transgender man, he accepted me and treated me as an equal. Not only that, but he introduced me to my connected partner Farrah, who just happened to be a transgender woman. Both of us, from the time that we arrived to the City of Disciples, never felt as though we were any different than any other disciple. The leader made sure of it."

Farrah continued. "I was embarrassed of who I was due to the treatment by not only my parents when I came out to them, but also by the rest of my family. My brother was the only one who was accepting of me. As a matter of fact, he's the one who introduced me to the leader and the City of Disciples. He trusted me to be there for his children. The leader will be missed."

Samantha and Lawerence chose to speak together as well. Juliet, Hawk and Sparrow chose to go up and whisper into Azril's ear, as if they only wanted him to hear what they had to say.

Once every disciple who wanted to speak had said what they wanted, Alpha stepped back up into position, with Xavier by her side. "As the leader has been released from the physical land, into the promised land, let's praise God for the promise of immortality. God of wisdom and leader of the promised land, please lead this disciple into the promised land as they have been released from the physical land. Watch over the disciples still remaining in the physical land and give them understanding, as they also wait for their release into the promised land. Give us the strength to continue to follow You, as well as the understanding as to why the leader was chosen to join You in the promised land. We are Disciples of God and we will appease You in worship."

"We are Disciples of God and we will appease You in worship," the others repeated.

The disciples all stood and prepared to take Azril back through the trail to the City of Disciples. Xavier grabbed Alpha and they pulled the wagon, with the duffle bags full of money, into a bushy area around the base of a group of four trees.

Just as the wagon was completely concealed, Xavier wrapped his arms around Alpha and Samantha peeped in between the trees at them. "Hey, are y'all coming?"

"Yeah, mom. We're coming. Alpha just needed a minute and asked me to wait with her," Xavier lied.

"Okay, well let's go," Samantha said, placing her hand on their backs and lightly pushing them toward the disciples.

Cory and Lawerence lifted the makeshift stretcher, where Azril's body had been placed, and they all walked toward the opening they had come through from the City of Disciples. Martin and Debora stepped through the bushes at the wall.

"Freeze! Get down on the ground!" several police officers yelled, as they emerged through the opening in the wall.

Cory and Lawerence gently set the stretcher down and both got down on their knees. As the rest of the disciples and children also lowered themselves down onto their knees, Alpha and Xavier turned and ran back to the nature preserve to hide.

They hid in the underbrush near the area where they concealed the money, both holding one finger vertically across their lips directly under their nose. They could hear the police traipsing around them, but remained as quiet as they could until they couldn't hear the police any more.

Xavier peeked through one side of the brush, as Alpha peeked through the other side. The police had retreated and the two eight year olds reemerged from the underbrush. They wandered around the area, finding the tents some of the disciples had stayed in the night before had been thrown around and were no longer standing.

"Do you know how to set up a tent?" Xavier asked Alpha.

"Of course I do. Now let's find a tent big enough for the two of us to stay separate until our connection ceremony," Alpha said, as they began looking through what would become their shelter for a while.

Xavier held up a two room tent and Alpha nodded. They both picked up the poles used to pitch the tent, as four dogs approached them.

Alpha held her hand out for the dogs to approach. "I think these are Buddy's puppies. I mean they are full grown dogs now, but I think these are the puppies that mom and dad brought over from the original City of Disciples."

"There's a story in the Disciples Doctrine about how God sent Buddy to the leader to be his companion and protector. Do you think God has guided Buddy's puppies to be our companions and protectors?" Xavier asked.

"That has to be it. We need to give them names, so we can stop calling them Buddy's puppies," Alpha told him.

"There are three girls and one boy. We can name them Buddy junior, Luna, Starla and Sunny," Xavier said, shrugging.

"That's perfect. Not only that, but they could help keep us safe until we find permanent housing," Alpha told him.

They found some snacks that they were sure the dogs could eat and fed them just a little bit before they headed off. The tent was secured in the wagon with the money. Alpha and Xavier each took turns pulling the wagon.

The dogs led them through the woods for months. Every night they would set up camp to sleep. Having the money helped them eat regularly as well as being able to feed all four of the dogs.

By the time Alpha and Xavier were in their tenth year, the dogs had managed to lead them back to the original City of Disciples that Azril and Omegra had set up. The three foot wall was still standing and the stump chair had been mostly taken over by termites.

They set up the tent and settled in for the long haul. If Azril and Omegra were able to live hidden in that neck of the woods for years, Alpha and Xavier were going to do the same.

About the Author

C. L. Conolly is an avid horror and true crime fan. Her novels are meant to bring attention to real world issues with a major gore focus. She attends several horror conventions and events each year in order to meet readers in person. To find out more, check out www.clconolly.com and follow on all social media platforms.

When C. L. Conolly isn't writing, she's relaxing at her country home with her husband, family and pets. She has one son, a daughter-in-law and two grandchildren.

Facebook - C. L. Conolly - Author
Instagram - C. L. Conolly
Twitter - @CLConolly
TikTok - @c.l.conolly
YouTube - @c.l.conolly